SANDY ASHER

Stella's Dancing Days

ILLUSTRATED BY KATHRYN BROWN

HARCOURT, INC.
San Diego • New York • London

www.harcourt.com

Library of Congress Cataloging-in-Publication Data
Asher, Sandy.
Stella's dancing days/Sandy Asher;
illustrated by Kathryn Brown.
p.   cm.
Summary: A charming kitten named Stella dances for the
family who owns her, but as Stella grows up, she dances
less and less, and everyone misses her dancing days—until she
has six kittens of her own who all love to dance.
[1. Cats—Fiction.]   I. Brown, Kathryn, 1955–   , ill.
II. Title.
PZ7.A816St   2001
[E]—dc21   00-8302
ISBN 0-15-201613-9

First edition
A C E G H F D B

Printed in Hong Kong

The illustrations in this book were done in watercolors and
pen and ink on Arches paper.
The display type was set in Contrivance.
The text type was set in Baskerville.
Printed by South China Printing Company, Ltd., Hong Kong
This book was printed on totally chlorine-free
Nymolla Matte Art paper.
Production supervision by Sandra Grebenar and
Pascha Gerlinger
Designed by Ivan Holmes

For the New Ones: Andrew, Bailey, Katie, and Natalie

–S. A.

For Layna and Wyatt

–K. B.

Stella was a kitten who loved to dance.

When the Tall One came to meet her,
Stella showed him her *grands jetés*,
and the Tall One grinned with delight.

When the Gentle One welcomed her home,

Stella performed pirouettes across the floor,
and the Gentle One was charmed.

When the Littlest One with the Loudest Voice
would not stop crying,
Stella and her tinkly ball
waltzed from room to room until, at last,
the Littlest One laughed.

And when the Fuzzy One with Floppy Ears
barked right in her face,
Stella did her best tumbles and flips,
then took a deep bow
that ended in an arabesque.

She and the Fuzzy One became fast friends,
and as they shared their busy days and cozy nights,
Stella grew up.

She discovered bugs in the garden that needed stalking,
patches of sunlight just her size,

and windowsills where she could sit
and watch the world go by.

She still danced now and then,
but only on special occasions.

"Stella is a fine cat," said the Tall One,
"but I do miss her dancing days."
"Stella is a beautiful cat," said the Gentle One,
"but I miss her dancing days, too."

"Stella is a *big* cat now," said the Littlest One,
"and I am a big boy!"

Stella did not miss her dancing days.
It was time for other things.
There were mice to send scurrying from the woodpile
and songs to sing with the neighbor cats
beneath the night sky.

One day, Stella began searching for a place
where she could be alone.
When she found it, she slipped away
and rested there.

"Where's Stella?" the Littlest One asked.
"Shh!" warned the Gentle One.
"Is Stella sick?" whispered the Littlest One.
"No," the Tall One told him. "She's fine.
  Let her be."

So Stella stretched out in her special place
and waited quietly, patiently,
for kittens of her own.

Soon she was busier than ever—
with kittens to clean, kittens to feed,
and kittens to keep safe and warm.

And when the time was right, the rest of the family
gathered to greet the New Ones.

There were six of them: three girls and three boys.
And they all loved to dance.